To all the kids in the world,
especially my beautiful daughter, Lena,
and to my mom,
for believing the artist in me

Special thanks to Laura

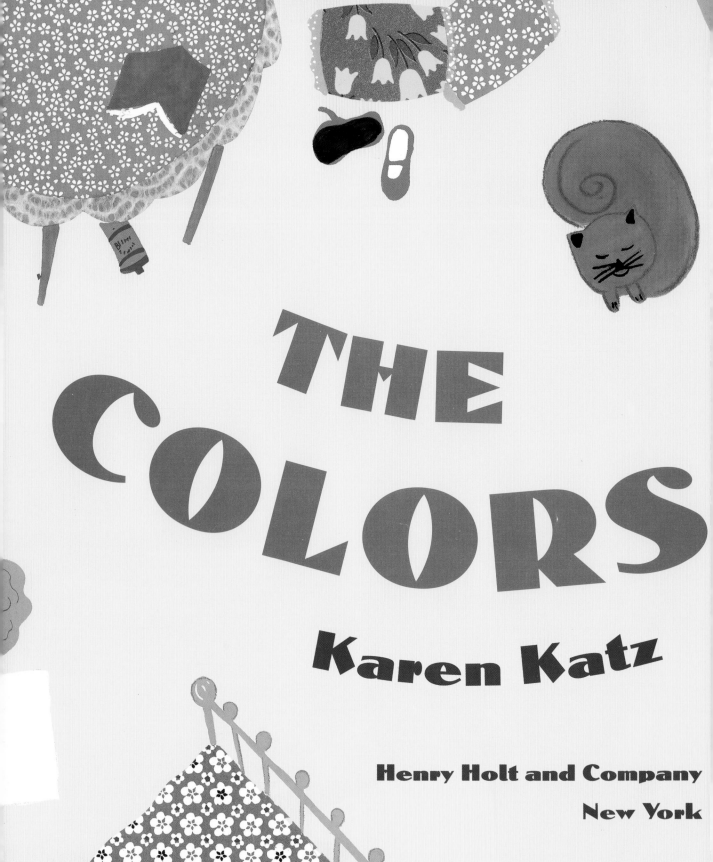

THE COLORS

Karen Katz

Henry Holt and Company

New York

My name is Lena, and I am seven.
I am the color of cinnamon. Mom says
she could eat me up.

My mom's the color of French toast. She's an artist.
Mom's teaching me how to mix colors. She says that
if I mix red, yellow, black, and white paints in the right
combination, I will have the right brown for a picture of me.
   "The right brown? But Mom, brown is brown," I say.
   "That's not so," Mom says. "There are lots of different
shades of brown. Let's take a walk. You'll see."

We go to the playground, where we see my friend Sonia.
"Sonia is a light yellow brown," Mom says.
"Just like creamy peanut butter," I say. "My favorite."

Isabella is chocolate brown, like the cupcakes we had for her birthday.

Lucy has skin that's peachy and tan.

My best friend, Jo-Jin, lives close to the
playground. Jo-Jin is the color of honey.

Two streets over, we meet my cousin Kyle.
His skin is a reddish brown, like leaves in fall.

Carlos and Rosita have brought their new puppy to the park. Carlos is a light cocoa brown. And Rosita's skin looks like butterscotch.

When we pass by the pizza parlor, Mom and I see Mr. Pellegrino flipping a pizza high in the air. He is the color of pizza crust, a golden brown.

My baby-sitter Candy is like a beautiful jewel,
bronze and amber. She looks like a princess.

Mom and I walk to the park to eat our lunch. "Look at everyone's legs, Mom—all the different shades."

After lunch we walk to Mom's favorite store, where Mr. Kashmir sells many different spices. He's the color of ginger and chili powder.

Up the street is my aunt Kathy's Laundromat. Aunt Kathy is tawny tan like coconuts and coffee toffee.

After our walk, my friends come over. We take our towels to the roof and lie in the sun. I think about everyone I saw today: Sonia, Isabella and Lucy, Jo-Jin and Kyle, Carlos and Rosita, Mr. Pellegrino and Candy, Mr. Kashmir and Aunt Kathy—each one of them a beautiful color.

My friends leave and I go downstairs. I am happy as I get out my paints: yellow, red, black, and white. I think about all the wonderful colors I will make, and I say their names out loud. Cinnamon, chocolate, and honey. Coffee, toffee, and butterscotch. They sound so delicious.

At last my pictures are done, and I've painted everyone.

"Look, Mom," I say. "The colors of us!"

SQUARE FISH
An Imprint of Macmillan

Henry Holt and Company, LLC, *Publishers since 1866*
175 Fifth Avenue, New York, New York 10010 [mackids.com]

Library of Congress Cataloging-in-Publication Data
Katz, Karen. The colors of us / Karen Katz.
Summary: Seven-year-old Lena and her mother observe the variations in the
color of their friends' skin, viewed in terms of food and things found in nature.
[1. Racially mixed people—Fiction.] I. Title.
PZ7.K15745Co 1999 [Fic]—dc21 98-47508

Originally published in the United States by Henry Holt and Company
First Square Fish Edition: September 2012
Square Fish logo designed by Filomena Tuosto
The artist used collage, gouache, and colored pencils to create the illustrations for this book.
mackids.com

ISBN 978-0-8050-5864-2 (Holt hardcover)
17 19 20 18

ISBN 978-0-8050-7163-4 (Square Fish paperback)
17 19 20 18 16

AR: 2.5 / LEXILE: 370L